TAPSTUDS

StickyGraphicNovels.com

Printed and distributed by
ComicMix, LLC.,
71 Hauxhurst Ave. Suite B
Weehawken, NJ 07086.
http://www.comicmix.com

Printed in USA.

Hardcover ISBN: 978-1-939888-84-6

SEXUAL DIPLOMACY

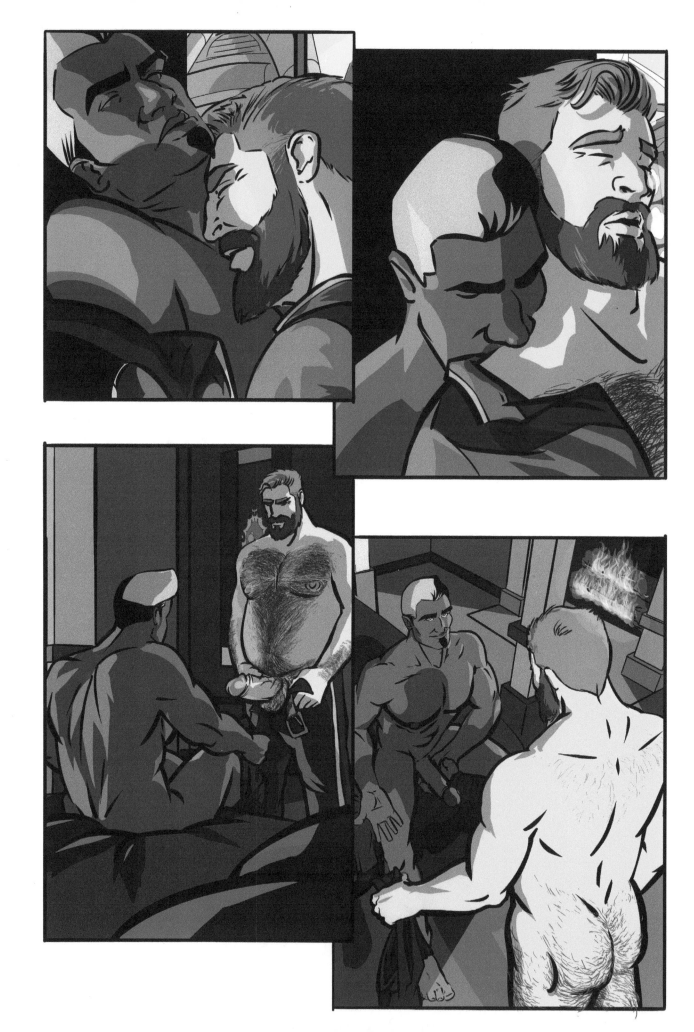

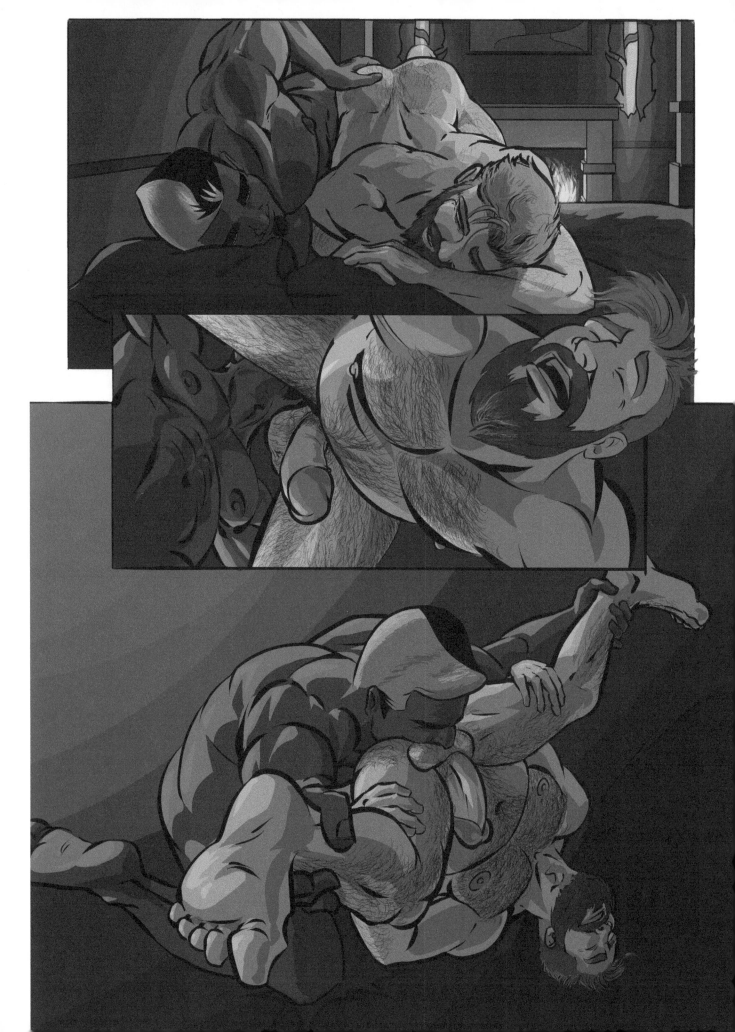

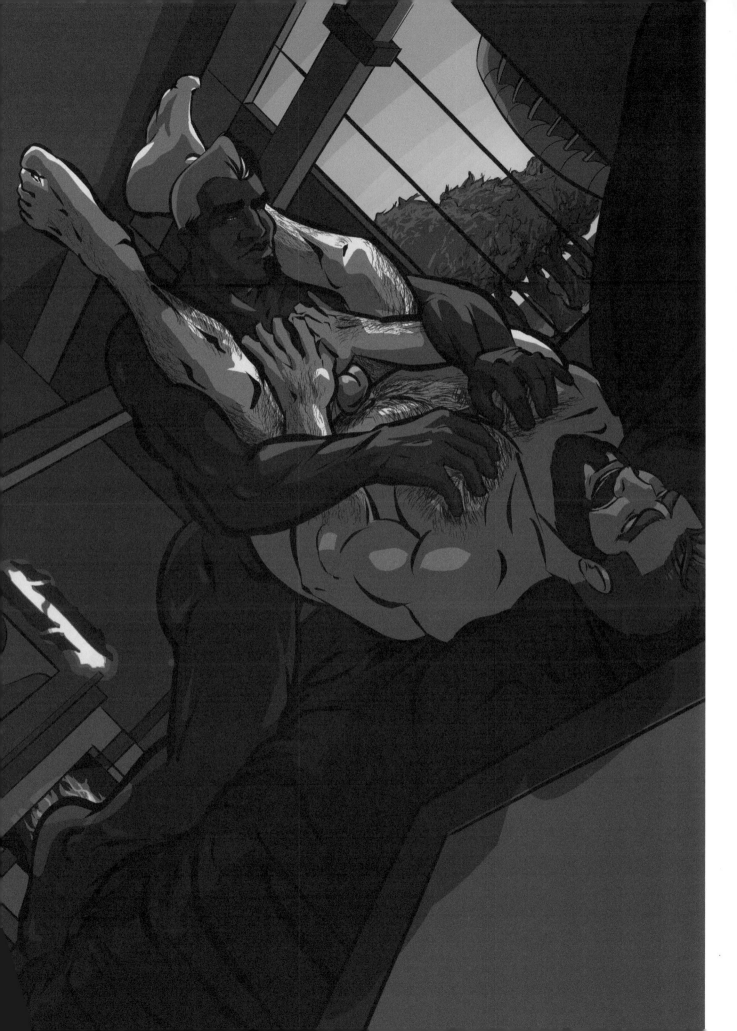

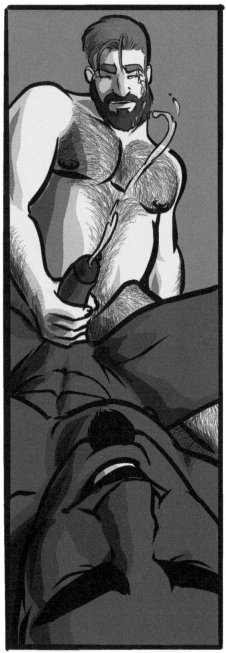

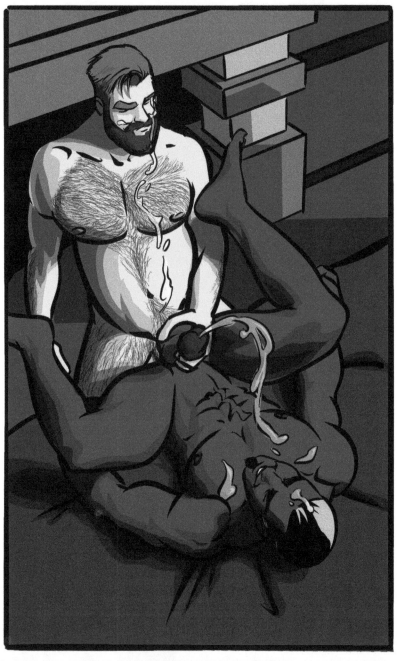

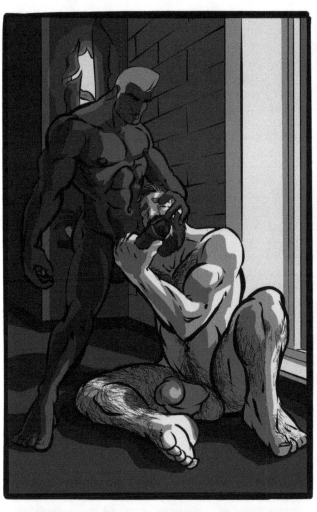

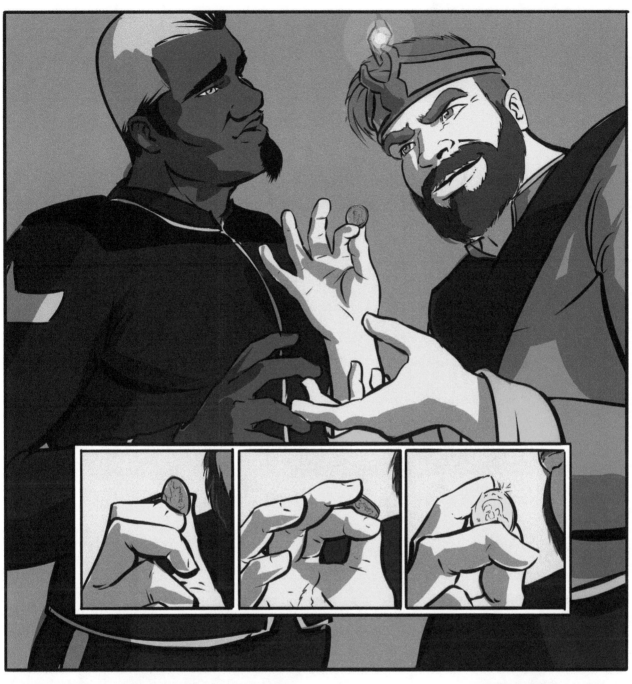

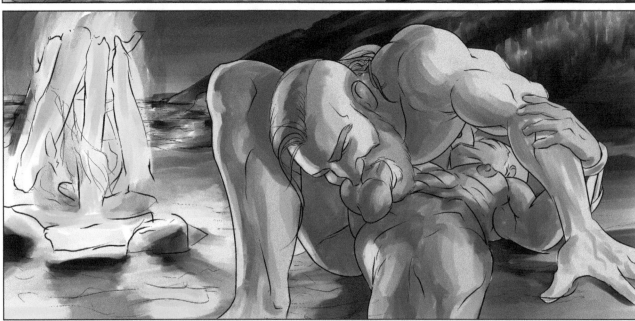

CHRONOFUCKING

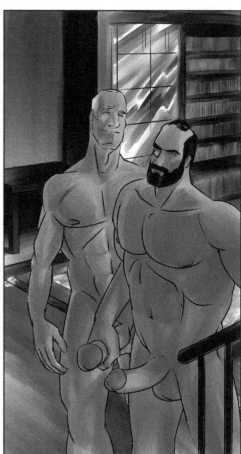

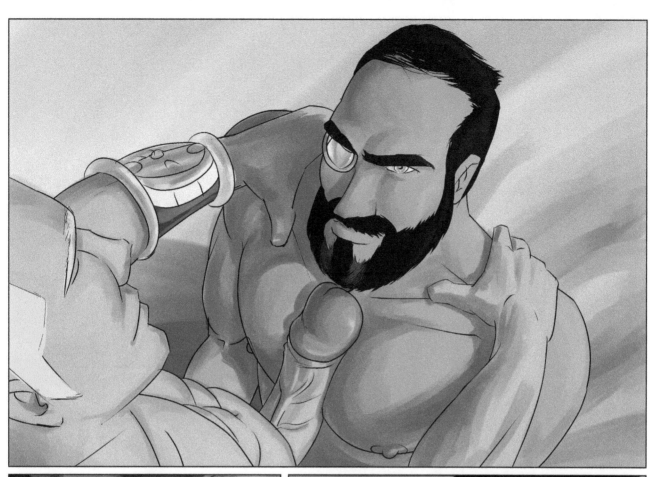

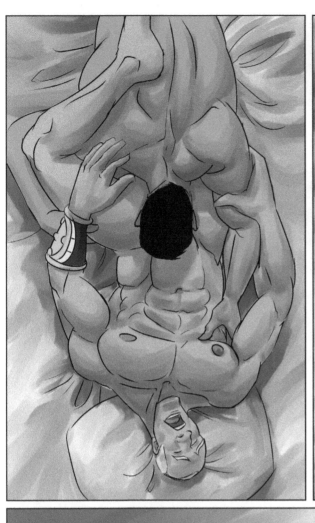
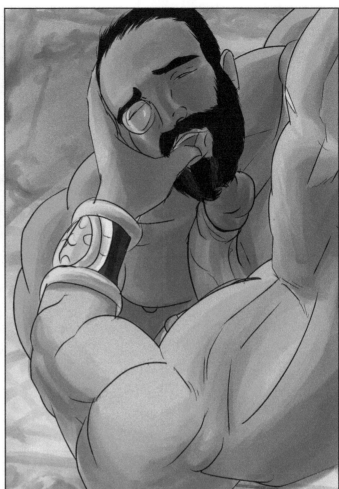

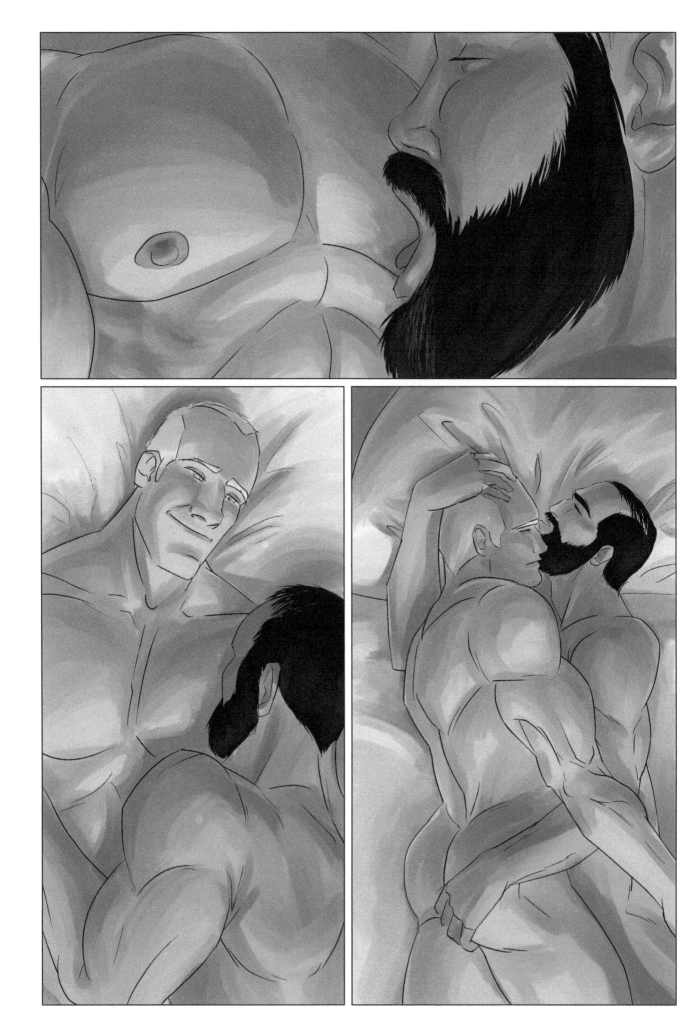

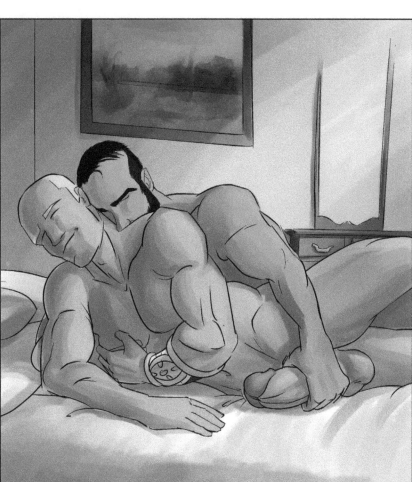

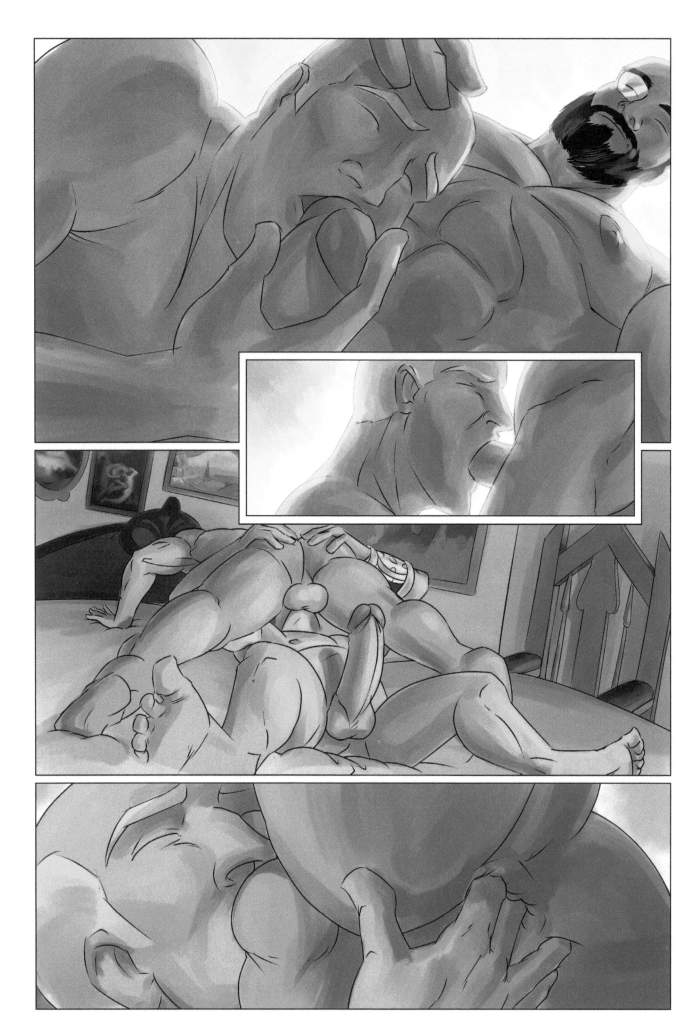

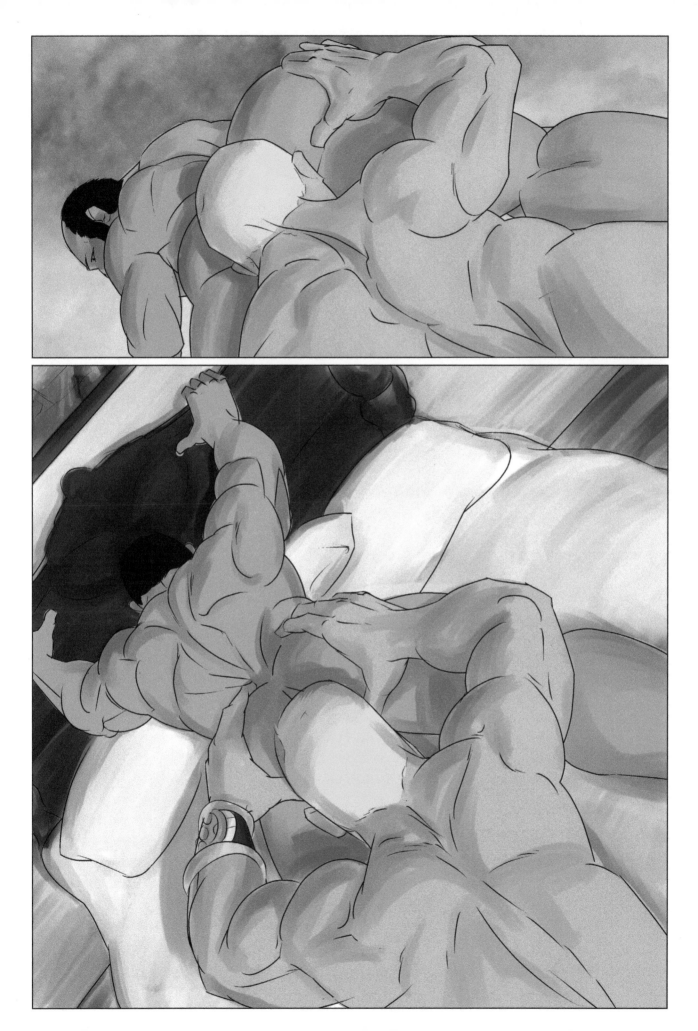

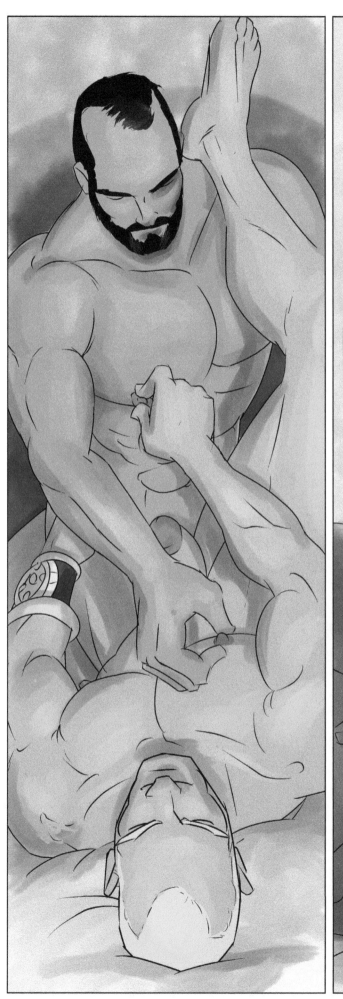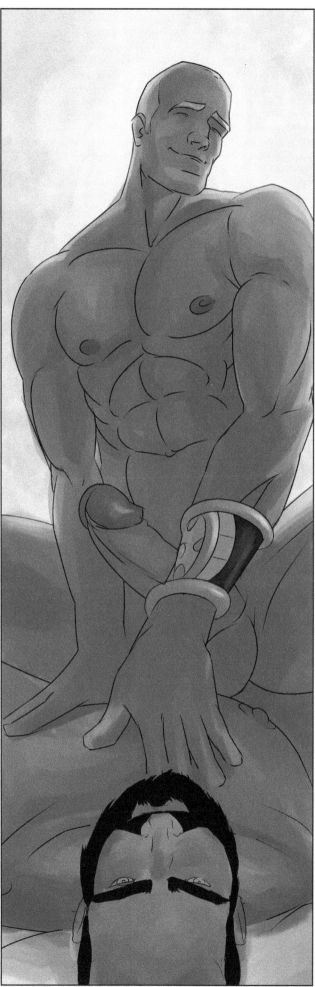

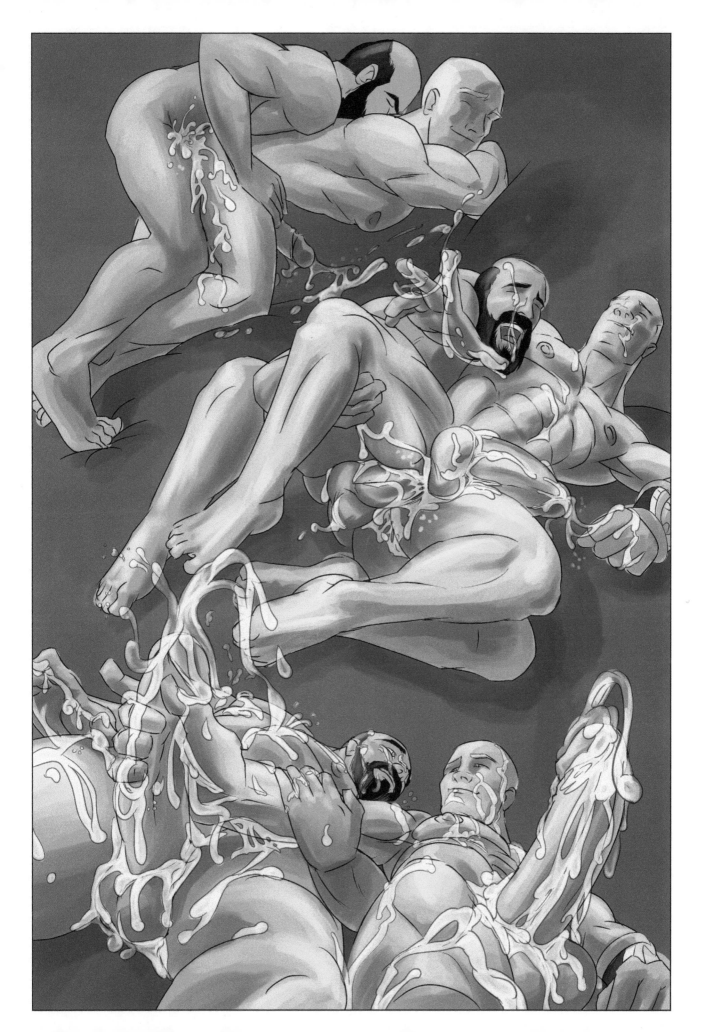

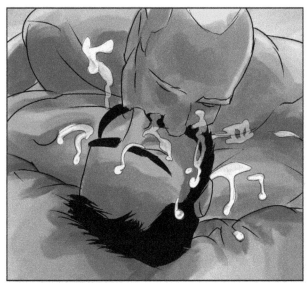

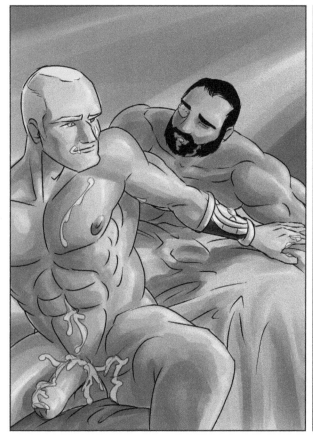
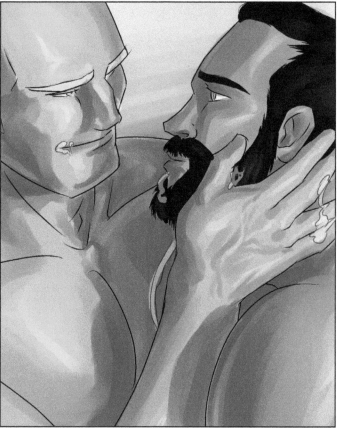

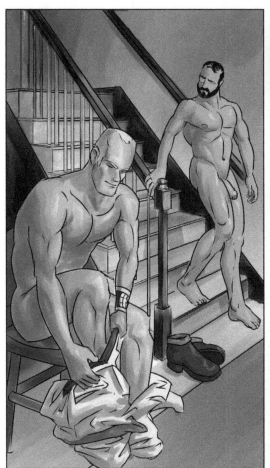

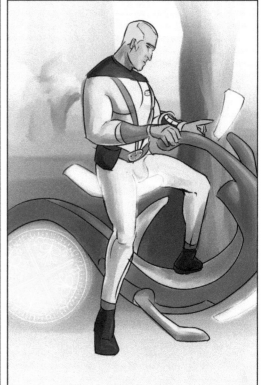

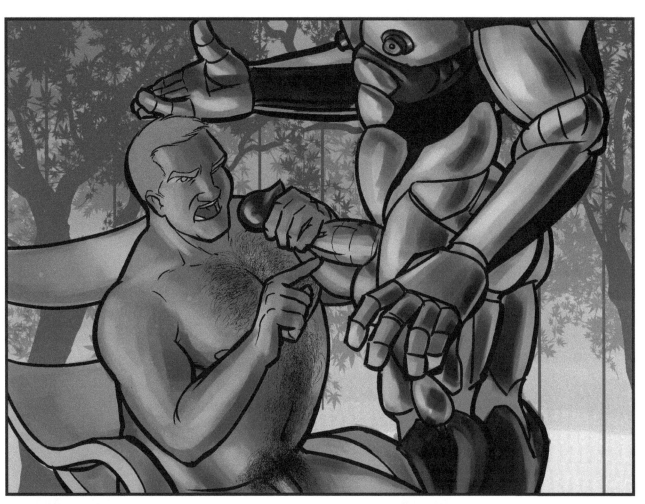

LOVE MACHINES

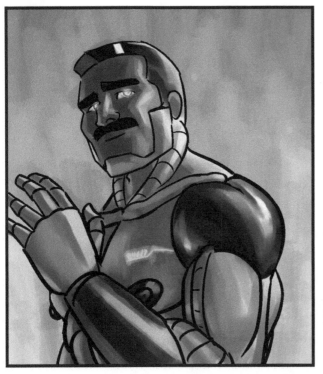

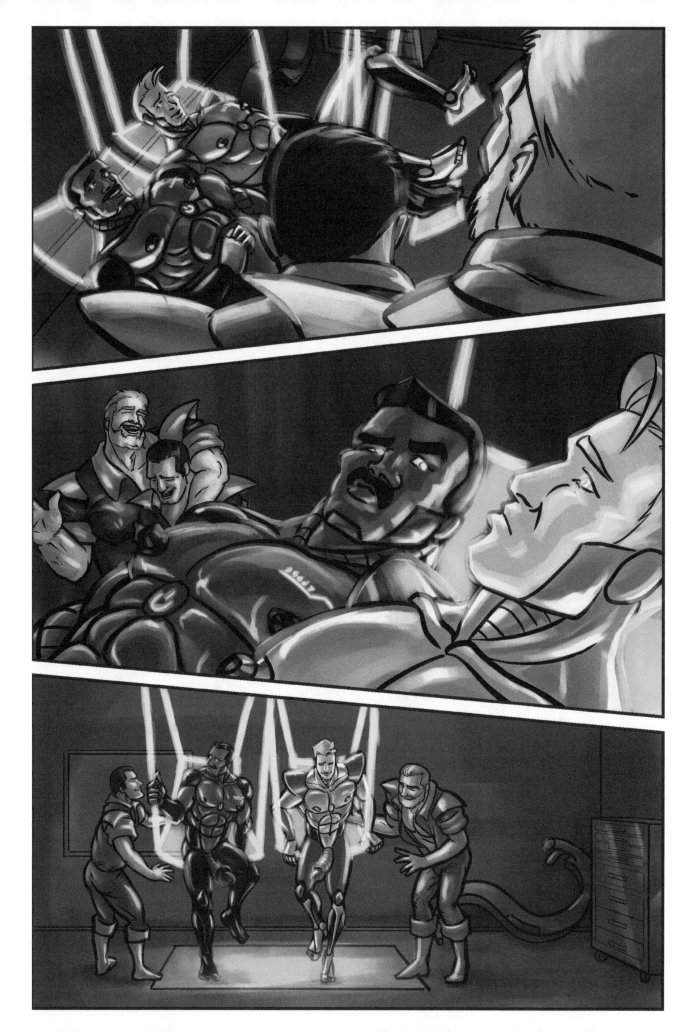

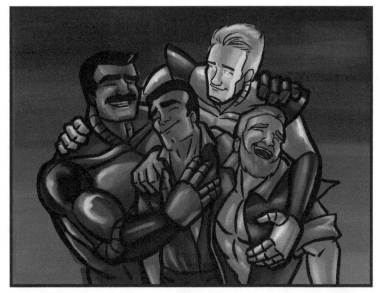

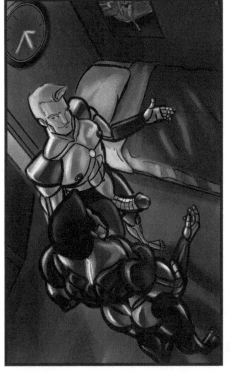

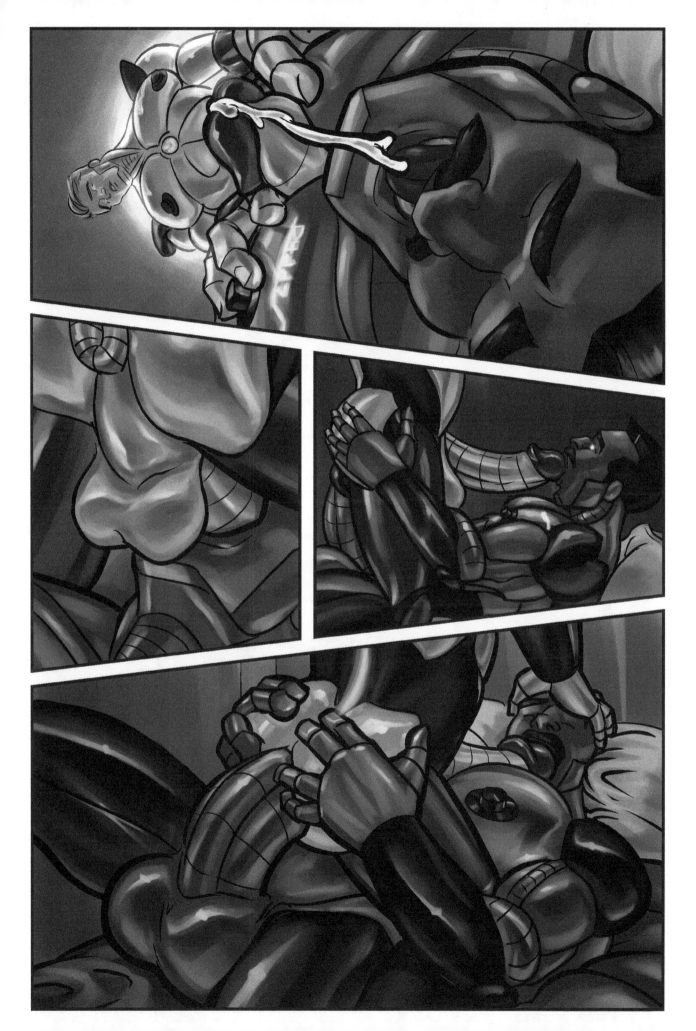

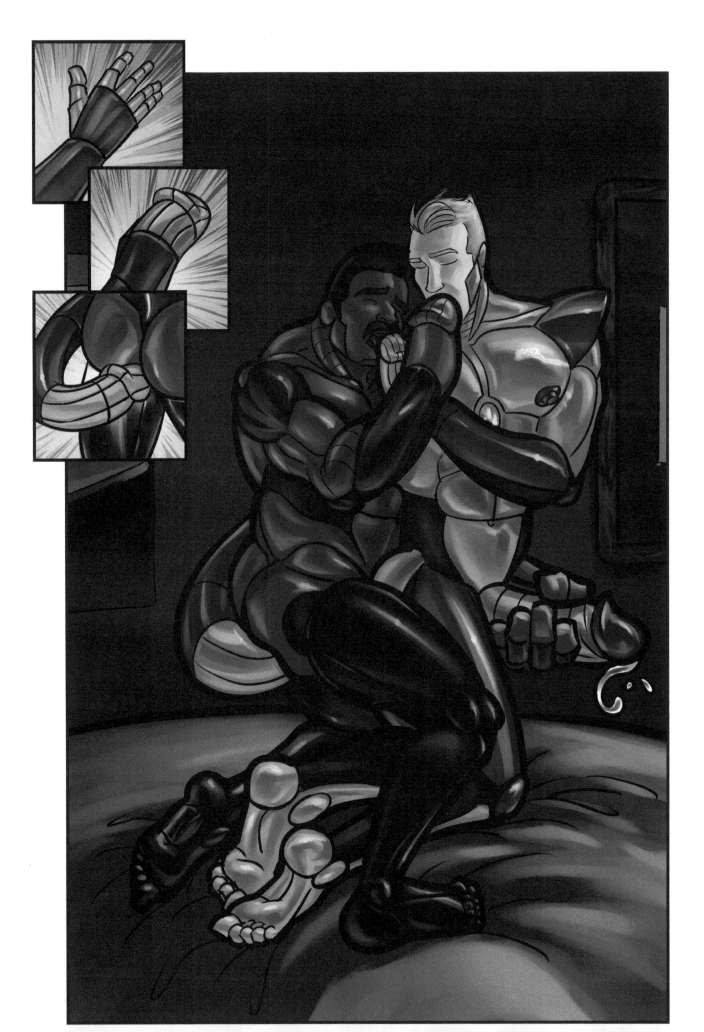

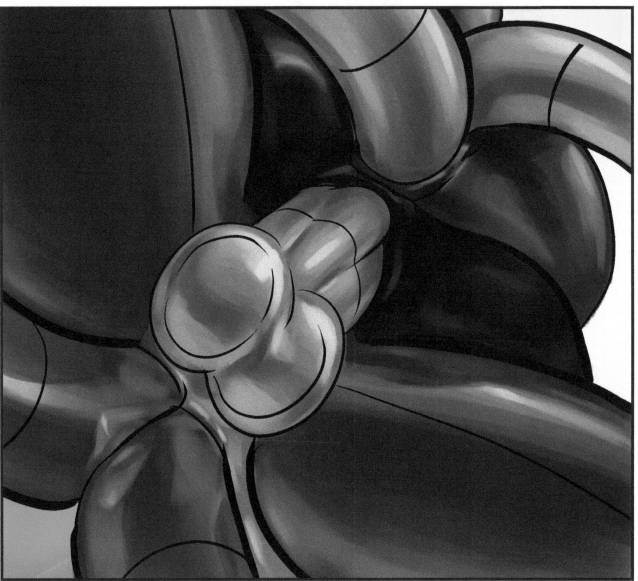

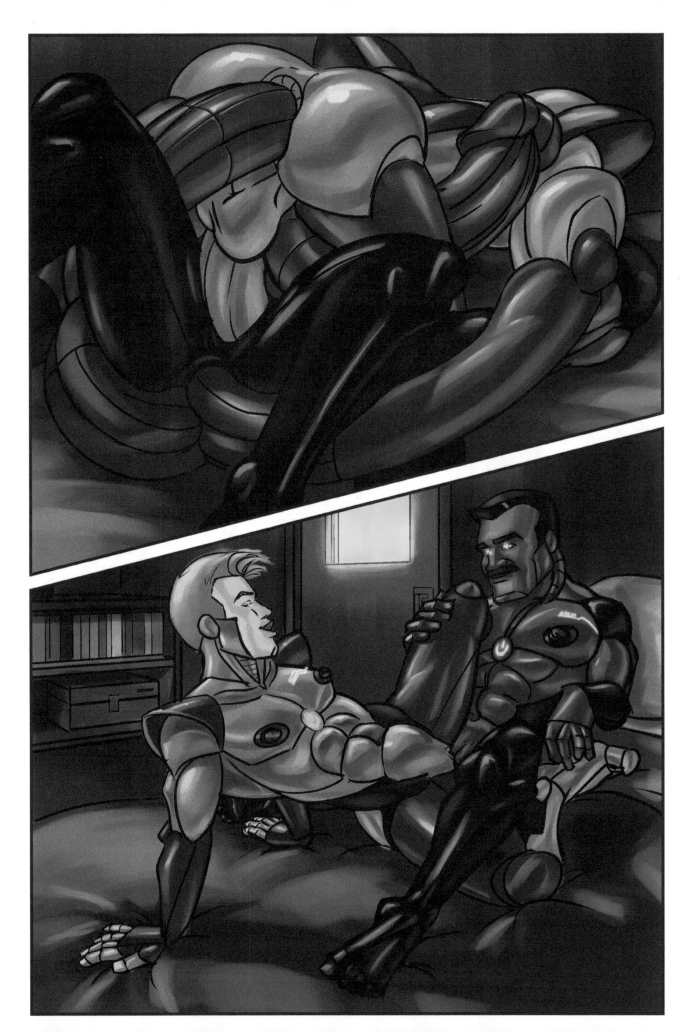

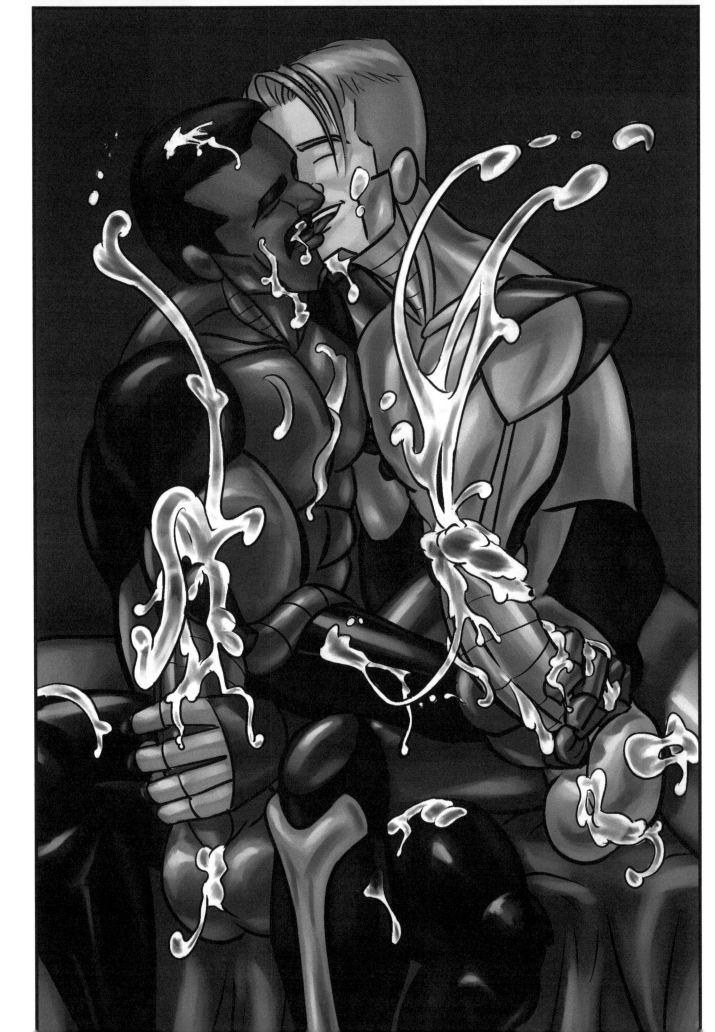

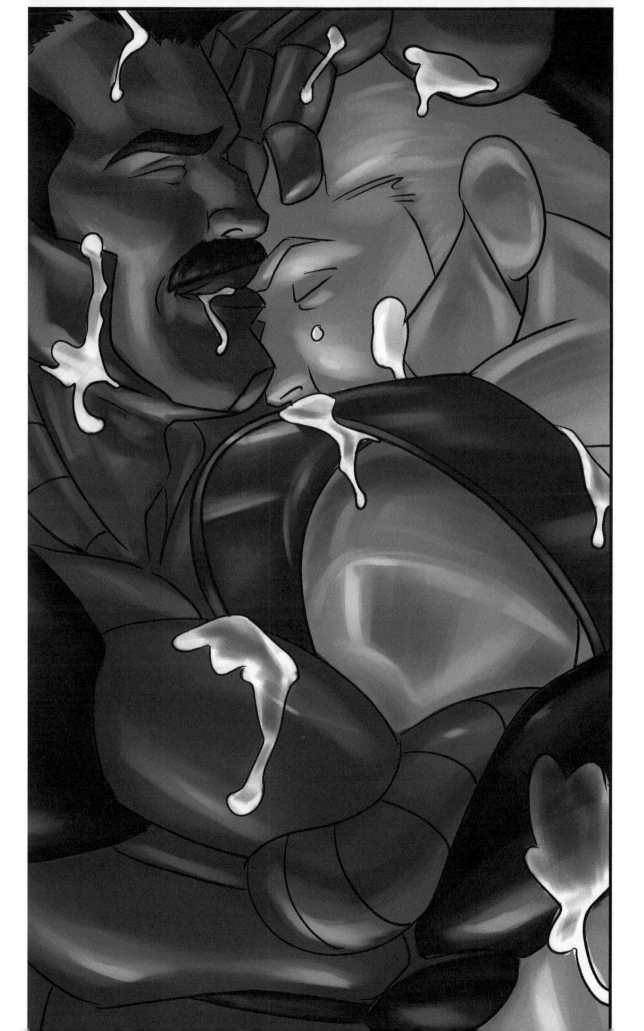

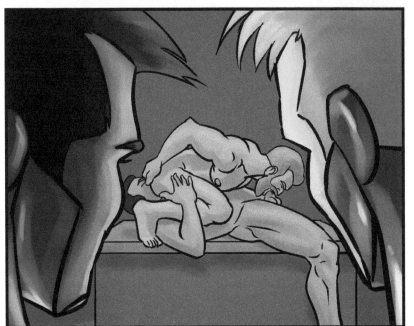

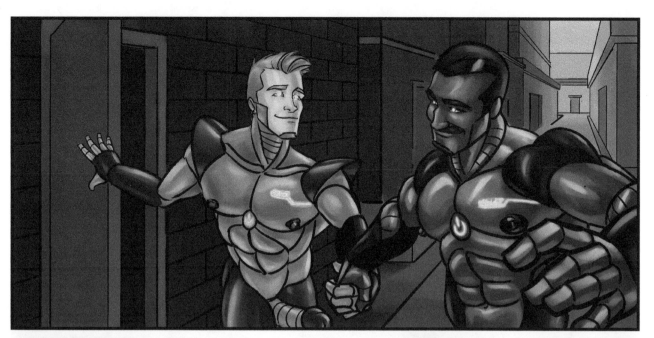

script/edits: Dale Lazarov
linework/colors: Dustin Craig

About The Authors:

Dale Lazarov is known as The Father of American Bara Comics and The Stan Lee of Gay as the writer, art director and licensor of Sticky Graphic Novels. Sticky Graphic Novels are wordless, gay character-based, sex-positive graphic novels for an international audience that are considered "a joyous expression of male/male sexuality that, while erotic, is neither grubby nor tasteless" (*The Novel Approach*). Since 2006, he has collaborated on 17 hardcover Sticky Graphic Novels and 43 digital editions with distinctive and evocative gay comics artists from around the globe. In his secret identity, he is Aldo Alvarez, Ph.D., and lives in Chicago.

Dustin Craig has a passion to create homoerotic comics and to tell powerful stories through his illustrations. Artists like Tom of Finland, Marc DeBauch, and Patrick Fillion inspired him to earn a B.F.A. in Comic and Sequential Imaging from Broadview Entertainment Arts University. *His Father* and *Nine Inch Ninjesus* comics are examples of his ability to create original and emotional stories with adult themes. He has had the pleasure and honor to collaborate with Dale Lazarov as the artist for TAPSTUDS. He currently works on his new comic series, *Starship Dominatrix*. Dustin and his partner, Glen, have been have been together for more than 14 years, and they have two adorable little puppies.